A Fate in the Woods

I'll Never Tell

Jessaka Nastalski

ISBN 978-1-62806-384-4 (print | paperback)

Library of Congress Control Number 2023911418

Published by Salt Water Media
29 Broad Street, Suite 104
Berlin, MD 21811
www.saltwatermedia.com

Cover designed by Salt Water Media using properly licensed stock imagery from istockphoto.com

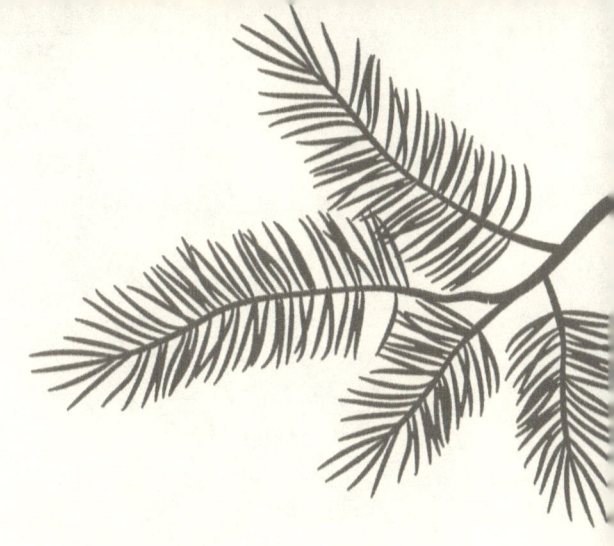

A Fate in the Woods

I'll Never Tell

to my students,
past, present and future,
for inspiring me

Introduction

Dear Readers,

As a Language Arts teacher for the past 23 years, I found it difficult to find high-interest stories that engaged young adult readers that may not necessarily LOVE to read. Fast-paced stories with shorter chapters and high-interest topics have proven to engage readers who may show reluctance to read.

You, my reluctant readers, are my inspiration. You have inspired me to create stories that will interest young adult learners and grab their attention. With varied sentence styles, strong voice and likeable, real characters, this story will naturally grab your attention and keep you reading until the end. The characters may be unreliable and unstable, but, boy, are they relatable.

For all of you whose ADHD makes it hard to comprehend, or the ones who are too 'busy' with life to pick up a book and be transported to another world, or for those of you who don't like reading because it is 'not cool' or for those of you who just don't gravitate toward reading, this book is for you.

Just try it. Take the first step and read the first page. You will be sucked in. You will want to keep reading. You will meet characters that you will like, and some you will not like. You will learn from their choices, mistakes, and experiences so you can navigate your own life in the right direction.

I am sure you will like the characters. I am certain you will read to the end so you can see if your judgments and assumptions about these characters are accurate. Once you have met Jess and Griff, you will want to get to know them better. Look for them in the prequel, *A Fate in the Woods: Before We Met*, and learn about their lives before they met on this fateful night.

Happy Reading,
Jessaka Nastalski

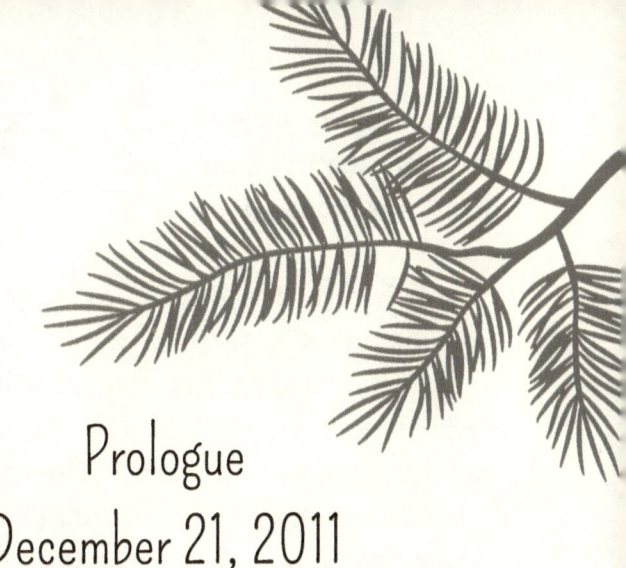

Prologue
December 21, 2011

I pushed through the darkness. The barren tree limbs and branches scraped and clawed at my face as I tried to push myself into the light. Away from this darkness, this cold, this craziness.

I didn't dare peek behind me. I could still hear the leaves crackling and twigs snapping as he tried not to make any noise following me.

I tried to move quickly but remained quiet. I tried to imagine myself as a panther, dark and sleek, stealthily finding my way through this blackness. But, instead, I felt my warm tears rolling down my cold, reddened cheeks and my breath was rasping in my chest, coming in bursts.

A twig snapped to my right, too close for me to continue to move.

Instead, I stood still, unmoving, behind the tree trunk, hoping my ragged breathing was quiet and my body was hidden.

Trembling, shaking, I prayed that he would move on. I prayed he would not see me.

I counted to forty-five and thought I heard a cracking come from the right, but further ahead of the tree behind which I was hiding, hopefully not losing this game of hide-n-seek.

I slowly turned and started to creep quickly, trying not to step on any twigs or trip or roll my ankle as the darkness enshrouded me and tried to wrap me in her dark embrace.

About twenty steps into my escape, I heard his raspy breathing and smelled the stench of his dirty clothing.

"It must not have been washed this week?" I remember thinking right as he silently grabbed me from behind, wrapping me in a bear hug. I could feel wool sleeves scratch my face as I twisted and turned, trying to escape. But he was too strong. His arms squeezed, like a constrictor. One arm found its way to my neck, closing around my throat like a wrestler choking out his enemy. It was smooth and taut, tightening like predator wringing the life out of its prey, rippling with muscle, constricting, pulling tighter.

I tried to pull his arms off, tried to kick free. I was gasping for air, like a fish out of water. I am sure my eyes were bulging from my head. At least they felt they were going to pop out at any second.

Was that the roadrunner on his wrist?

And then, it all just went black.

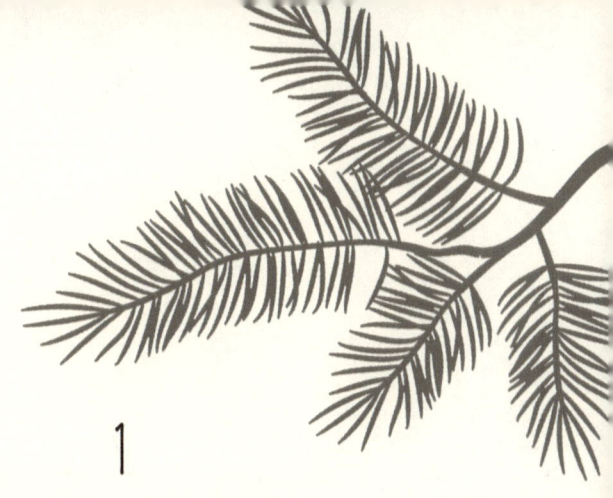

1

September 19, 2011

Not sleeping was an ugly side effect of watching your mom die. Laying there, staring at the ceiling, heavily aware that my mom was dying in the next room, one breath away from dying, was becoming the nightly norm. I don't know what I was thinking, but one night I decided that I should go for a walk. I thought walking through the moonlit woods would help ease my insomnia and help me sleep. A walk through the woods seemed like a good idea so I wouldn't be alone.

So, I grabbed the leash and, tossing the ball through the sliding door, she ran into the night, ready to go for a walk. I leashed her up and headed into a night that was going to change my life.

2
October 3, 2011

There's nothing like witnessing your mom die. Like, really watching the life drain out of her body, leaving her a shell of a human, barely able to take a breath. Her once round, smiling face with pink cheeks and long lashes from the carefully applied coats of mascara had shrunken. Her cheekbones had taken over her sunken face, a pale gray replacing the pinks of her cheeks and a frown replacing the smile that used to grace her lips.

Her long, blonde curls started thinning, left behind like little clues leading to her death. I would find them on the pillow, chair, or floor- anywhere she had laid her head. Her sparkling blue eyes dimmed and faded as death slowly crept over her body and into her mind. And her strong, muscular physique that had only endured forty years of life, carried a child and battled this disease had shrunken, been broken. She appeared more skeletal with every day that passed. Her cheekbones protruding from her darkened, shrunken sockets were a ghastly sight.

The physical withering was hard to stomach, but the smell, that smell, was the worst. The smell that took over our house was that of bile, sweat and fear. It was the stench of extreme sadness and death. It plagued my nostrils. Even as I tried to escape the sights and smell of my mother's death, the smell of my mother's slowly rotting body invaded my nostrils and deeply penetrated my nose. I caught whiffs of death no matter where I was.

Sitting in math class...there's the smell of death.

Walking down the cereal aisle...there's the stench of my mom's death.

Going for walk in the woods...there's the repugnant smell of dying flesh, leaving me retching on the trail.

That was hard for me after her death-trying to get the smell of death from the house. No amount of bleach, air freshener, candles or room spray could extinguish the smell of my mother's death. It's as if it seeped into the walls , carpets, floors and furniture. It had seeped into the souls of the house.

So, it shouldn't have been surprise that her death had permeated my father's soul as well.

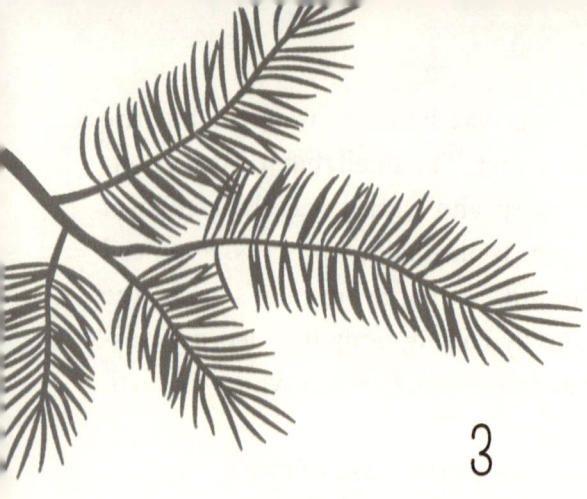

3
September 19, 2011

I first saw him when I was walking Meubles. She had so much energy and loved walking through the woods, sniffing along the trodden path, chasing birds, deer and other scents invisible to me. She and I had walked this path many times-too many to count on my hands and feet and all of her paws.

On this particular day, for some reason, she had started sniffing to the right of the path. Now, at this point in the summer the trees were lush with green growth and the berries were in full bloom. So, Meubs could sense things I could not see. It was also after one in the morning so it was rather dark out here.

She started pulling me from the path and a low growl started in the back of her throat, almost coming from her chest, low and guttural. I had never heard my lovable dog make this sound before.

"No way girl...are you crazy?" I stopped walking and tried to pull her back using both hands on the leash. She continued to lean forward, making that unfamiliar low growling sound, pulling me deeper into the thick bush and berries.

"Come on. Let's go!" I barked at her.

And then I saw what she was growling at; or rather who she was growling at. There was a torn blue tarp and some rope.

There was someone sleeping under a makeshift tent made of bungee cords of some sort. He (I don't know how I knew, but I knew it was a "he" from my first glimpse) was on his back with what looked to be an opened shoe box covering his face. Then again, maybe it was his clothing that made me think "he".

He had on faded blue jeans, like typical Levi's jeans that any Regular Joe would wear. And he had on a wool coat. It was September and he was wearing this dark gray wool coat that showed almost half of his forearms above his folded hands on his chest. He had dark hair on the part of his left arm that was facing me. I could see it from where I was and remember thinking, "With all that hair on his arm, he really does not need that wool coat!"

Now, all of these observations came within a matter of five seconds. And then all hell broke loose.

Either the primitive part of his animal brain kicked in because he sensed movement or maybe he heard Meubles's growl or felt her presence, but he sprang up from his sleep in one quick movement. I mean, like, jumped from lying flat on his back with his face covered to on the balls of his two feet, head swiveling and arms up (I can still see the arm hair), ready to fight.

Meubles charged. He screamed. He turned. He jumped.

He tried to reach for the branch above him and he missed-fell flat on his back, screaming in shock, pain, disbelief once again. At this point, Meubles was barking wildly and pulling and tugging on his wool coat sleeves, as he shielded his face from my dog. He was trying to roll onto his side and protect his face as Meubles kept pulling and tearing at his coat.

"Stop! Please! Get OFF!" he was yelling, trying to roll over and protect his face.

I finally found command of my legs again and started sprinting toward the entangled throwdown happening in front of me.

"Meubles! Get off him!" I screamed as my voice came back. "Get off girl!" I got hold of her collar and gave her a yank.

As soon as she was off him, he shot up and backed away.

"What the h...?!" he yelled, "What was that? Why did your dog...Jesus...damn...am I bleeding?"

"No. I'm sorry. No. You're ok, I think. You look okay. I'm sorry. I'm so sorry," I managed to stammer.

His hands found his face, his chest, his head, his hairy arms. They scanned all over his body, looking for bites, blood, injury. He found none.

"I am so sorry," I managed to apologize, once again.

"It's okay," he said, "I...I...just..." he turned away, his hand going through his hair.

"Look, it's all good," I said as I backed away, holding my dog at arm's length, since she was still growling at him. "I'm so sorry. I won't say a word," I promised, and I meant it, as I walked into the darkened night.

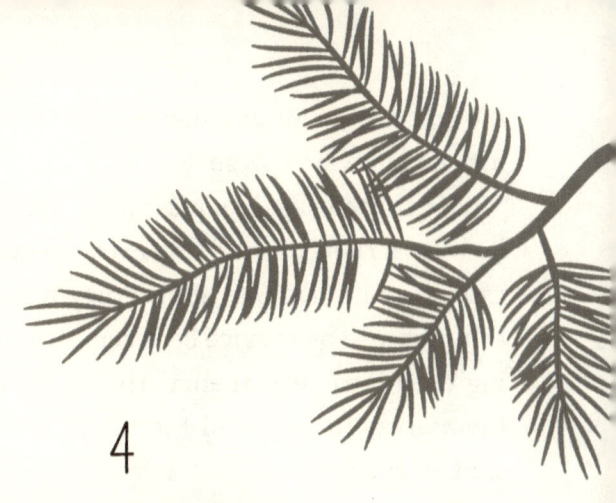

4

October 16, 2011

Watching your mother lose her battle with death was hard to do, but simultaneously watching your father watch the woman he loves get robbed of life was excruciating.

He took longer than she did, of course, since he started dying the minute the diagnosis came in. The man I knew as my father died the moment he heard the words from the doctor.

His dance with death was slow at first, but they picked up their dance as death's grasp tightened on my mother's skeletal body. He tried to be strong for her, for me, for us. It started with cracks in his soul, fractures really, that soon spider-webbed into broken pieces. I tried to help rebuild those fractures, I really did, but once the fractures widened and spread, his chances of ever being whole again were shattered.

I could see these fractures; I think even before he knew they were there. His badge of courage that he wore shielded him from most prying, judgmental, saddened eyes of friends and family. But my eyes spotted these threads of breakage, the spindles of his splintering heart obvious to me long before he knew he was shattered.

He started sagging, his whole body and face looked as if he was carrying around fifty extra pounds, which was not the case since he had lost about forty pounds from his already thin frame. The crevice between his brows was slowly delving itself into permanency. His circles darkened and etched themselves further and further down his face, toward his sunken cheeks.

His once bright white hair had yellowed and dulled, reflecting the lack of care he was applying to himself. It was thinning and lifeless, kind of like all the people in my house.

"How are you, Dad?" I'd ask.

"Getting by," or "Hanging in," became his go to responses as he blindly walked by me, not even noticing when I chopped my hair to chin length.

"Love you!" I would call after him, getting a wave or grunt in response, raising his right hand, not bothering to even turn around and see me.

Then he would be off to check on her. If he wasn't sitting by her bedside or tending to her, he was locked in his office. And I would be left standing there, pretending life was normal for a girl my age. You know, watching your dad watching your mom die as he slowly loses his grip on reality was normal, right?

So, the nightly strolls continued. Eventually, I left Meubles at home because she never really warmed up to Griff. She always growled, with her neck hair standing on end. So, I traveled to Griff's alone at night, trying to escape my reality.

5

December 3, 2011

Sitting in the cafeteria at lunchtime is like lunching in the jungle with a group of predatory beasts preying on the smaller, weaker, isolated beings trying to eat before they can be pounced upon by the stronger, more dominant creatures.

I was lucky enough to have three others in my crew. We were a tight-knit group that was stronger when we were together. There were more isolated, weaker kids to pick on besides the four of us.

"So, I saw him in that tent thing again," Tyler was saying to Jax.

They were standing right next to me and my crew. We were basically invisible to these two since they only paid attention to the 'cool' kids, and we certainly did not fall into that category. We could have been dancing a jig and they would not have seen us. We seeped into the tables. We were one with the bench. We were basically teenage superheroes who had the power of invisibility in this jungle.

"Where?" Jax asked. "The woods? Near the bike path? Past the bridge?"

My heart dropped into my stomach with a thud. They knew where he lived. My cheeks grew hot. My palms were sweating. My heart raced in my chest, and I was certain that everyone in the room could hear it slamming into my rib cage.

Of course, we were not talking at our table. Kayleigh was reading. Elsie was doodling some amazing sketches and Saryn was writing some music for a new song she was developing for the guitar. I was making a new playlist, so I had my air pods in. It appeared that I was listening to the music since I kept drumming my fingers on the table to an imaginary beat. This was the perfect set-up for eavesdropping on them.

"Yeah," Tyer replied, "It was that blue tarp thingy, past the bridge."

"Where we saw him before?" Jax interrupted, shifting his weight from foot to foot.

"Yup, he has to live there," Tyler stated, calm as could be. "We have seen him there three times now."

"Ok," Jax agreed, bouncing from foot to foot, "We have to do this soon, like really soon."

Tyler grinned. "What? Are you getting nervous that this won't work?"

"Nah," he quickly replied, "I just want this to be over." He turned and scuttered away, back to the cool table. Tyler turned slowly, his eyes settling on mine for longer than a beat. It was almost like he had tried to find my eyes in this jungle. He held my stare for three seconds and then he grinned and walked away, following Jax.

"What was that all about?" I wondered to myself. "What are they planning on doing?"

6

November 24, 2011

"So, what's it like?" I asked him, while we walked toward the creek. It had been about two months since I had stumbled upon Griff and I was happy to have a friend like him. I could talk to him about anything.

"What's what like?" he asked me, smiling that gorgeous smile, even though I was pretty sure we both knew what I was talking about.

"Living out here," I said, stopping and spreading my arms over my head, twirling to add emphasis to being 'out here' in the woods. The only thing that would have made that moment more magical would have been if birds landed on my arms and chipmunks, squirrels and butterflies scuttled up to me as I twirled.

He seemed to ponder that for a moment. "Well, it is just what I need," he paused and started walking again to catch up to me. "Is it scary at times? Yes! Is it cold? Yes! Is it hot? Yes! But it is just what I need in my life."

I turned and walked backwards, looking at him, taking

him in. His lips were parted a bit, his cheeks were flushed with pink from the walk and his eyes were golden in the sun-light. He was breath-taking. He was gorgeous.

"What you need?" I asked, "What is it that someone like you needs?" I teased, smiling and flipping my hair, slowing down just a bit so he could step closer to me.

"What I need is for you to stop walking, especially back-wards," he replied with his hands on his hips, feigning that he was catching his breath, his legs spread, hunched over at his waist.

"I don't think so," I responded and turned back to walking in front of him, swaying my hips this way and that as I walked on. "I am a pretty independent girl," I called over my shoulder.

I caught sight of him catching up to me, closing the space between us.

"I can tell that," he said. "I would not doubt it with the way you smashed right into my life." He stopped and looked like he wanted to say more but didn't want to say more. And then he started walking ahead of me.

After a moment of stunned silence, I started walking and tried to catch up to him.

"I'm sorry," I said even though I wasn't sure what I was apologizing for. Was it what I had said about his life? Or was I sorry for walking deeper into the woods? Or that my dog had attacked him when we first met? I wasn't sure, but I knew I felt sorry for him.

"What are you sorry for?" he asked, as if he was able to read my mind.

We slowed down, as we rounded the ridge. His eyes looked so sad despite the smile that he had on his lips.

I stumbled over my response, "I don't know…I just…I am just sorry…for life. For both us though…it's just not fair."

"Don't worry about what is fair for me," he eased.

"I'm not talking about your life. I am talking about how unfair my life is," I surprised myself with this daring declaration.

"Your life?" he asked, stopping our slow pace as we climbed the ridge, with concern in his eyes and disbelief in his voice. "What is unfair about your life?"

"My mom is dying," I blasted out in one breath. Then I took a deep breath and said, softer, "My mom is dying… and…I am watching it happen…and my dad is falling apart, dying in his own way."

He looked as though he was in complete shock. He stood, still, his mouth gaping open a bit, with tears swelling up in his eyes. And in the next second, he had his arms wrapped around me.

"I am so sorry," he said as he squeezed me in a tight hug. "I can't imagine that."

I lost count of how long he held me. I know that when I pulled myself away from his arms, my face was wet with tears and my snot had dripped onto his coat.

"Thanks," I managed to utter. "I haven't told anyone that yet. In fact, I think that's the first time I ever spoke those words out loud."

"Thank you for trusting me with this, Jess," he smiled.

I couldn't believe I had uttered those words, that I had actually admitted them out loud to the universe. I had told Griffin my secret. I had let it out. What would happen now that the universe had heard my admission? Would the universe speed up the process now that I had whispered the words into the air? I was hoping, sadly, regrettably, that maybe it would speed up death's overpowering victory over my mother so I would not have to watch her wither away, fade away into nothing, right before my eyes.

We started walking up the ridge again and he reached out and took my hand. It felt so warm, so safe, so right. I could not believe that I had shared this with anyone, let alone the homeless kid I stumbled upon in the woods a few weeks ago.

Which was worse? Me watching my mom die or him living out here without one?

7

December 18, 2011

"Honey, you ok?" he would ask me. I heard it about a million times. But, those million times were far in the past.

He had not asked me that question for fourteen weeks and three days. Yup, I was keeping count. That's a long time to go with your dad not asking if you are ok. This is especially harder if your mom started dying about eight weeks ago.

Eight long weeks of Dad and I living together, barely speaking more than a grumble or mumble being shared between us. It's not that I didn't try. I would ask, "Dad, how are you?" or "Dad, how are you feeling?" or "Dad, are you ok?"

He would barely respond. Maybe I would get a forced smile, a nod, an occasional thumbs up and sometimes I would get a grunt. This new form of communication took some time to get used to. It was a very quiet eight weeks.

Everything really shifted on Death Day. It was like he had been sucked into a black hole of sadness when she took her last breath. He had not recovered since that day. He was depressed and he was doing this whole depression thing well. He was all in.

I'm talking sunken cheeks, deeply creviced circles under his eyes that were almost always red from crying. His brow was furrowed into a scowl, frowning every glance I took of him.

As he sat in his brown recliner, rocking slowly, I would steal glances of him. Where did his glow go? When did he fade into this sad creature? He had 'died' long before my mom did. But that was unavoidable. It couldn't be helped. He loved her so much. His heart literally was breaking in front of me as he watched her slip closer to death's grip.

And, now, he was a shell of a human, existing because he had to-apparently for me. I guess he, and many other adults, felt I was in better care with him. They thought that me watching my mother die while watching my father lose his mind was a healthy thing for a teen.

I know differently. I know that living here, watching death take its toll, was not a good place for a teen. The walls breathed the stench of death, and you could make no mistake that death had settled upon our house.

How could someone possibly think it was healthy for me to be living here while death's talons clawed and ensnared my parents? How was I to know I would not be next?

8
December 5, 2011

"BEEEEEEEEEEPPPPP!" and with that, we poured into the hallways, like fish set free from a net.

If you haven't seen a high school hallway for a while, let me help you remember what it is like.

It's like the Savannah at 3 am. Or the Amazon at midnight. But it is just a Wednesday at 12:14 class change. There are some beasts that are finding their pack, some that are searching for their prey and others looking to camouflage. Some chose to travel in packs, and some traveled alone. Some were ready to engage, agitated, easily excited while others were on the defensive, trying to survive the walk without getting insulted or injured.

So, here I was, in the hallway, walking toward my next class. Kayleigh and Saryn were in Art now and Elsie had PE, so I was walking the third-floor halls alone.

I heard, "Maybe we should do it this weekend."

It sounded like Jax, so I had to sneak a look. I turned and caught a glimpse of Jax and Tyler, walking behind me. I quickly turned back around.

"Yeah, I think we need to do it sooner rather than later," Tyler responded. "Are we for sure taking it?"

"I think we should. Everyone knows it's his staple piece. He is always wearing that stupid thing," Jax continued, "If we are going to make this work, we need to do it soon. We need for them to think it was him that did it."

What were they talking about? I knew, but I didn't know. I kept walking toward history classroom 008. I wanted to hear more, but I was passing 004 now.

"Well, we know where his house is, if you want to call it that," Jax chuckled.

"Yeah, it's past the bridge, off the bike trail. You walk a bit, but you can't miss the blue tarps," Tyler added.

I knew they were talking about Griff, but what were they going to do?

"He always goes for a walk around 7:00. We can probably grab it then," Jax offered.

"He will probably be wearing it, dummy," Tyler pointed out.

"You're right," Jax agreed. "We should probably take it when he's sleeping then. We have to make it look like he left it behind, maybe rip it a bit, make it dirtier than it already is."

They were talking about his coat. Why would they take his coat from him? What if they were setting him up for something? What were they planning?

What did they have in store for Griff?

9

December 9, 2011

Talk about hard. The hardest day of my life so far was Death Day. The Day of Her Death. The Day She Left Me- Forever. I thought seeing her crawl closer and closer to death every day was hard, but this, this was damn near impossible.

Literally seeing your mom's last breath, the last time she inhaled sweet life and did not exhale was world-shattering. I kept watching, hoping to see her exhale that last breath, but she never did.

"Please breathe out, Mom...please, please, please breathe out," I begged, silently as my dad and I sat on either side of her bed. She was propped up on three pillows, as if elevating her would bring her closer to the living, make her more comfortable. She had the blue and white striped blanket pulled under her armpits, her arms by her sides.

Of course, her eyes were closed. They seemed to be closed for most of the last two weeks. I had not seen my mother's eyes open for two weeks.

So, when she never exhaled, I just about choked on my own breath. Who chokes on air? My mom was not breathing anymore, and I was choking on her expelled air of Death. I must've screamed. I must've cried. I must've been the one moaning. Because I looked up and saw my dad kiss her forehead…just like that. He stood over her, kissed her forehead, turned away and walked out of the room.

I don't know how much time passed, but I raised my head from my mother's stiffened body and had tears and drool on the blanket. The room was now darkened since no lights were on and the sun had set. I had been here for a while.

I walked out of the room and called for my dad.

"Dad?" I called, "Dad, where are you?"

There was no response to my calls.

I looked outside and saw his car was gone.

My mother's dead body was in her room and my father was nowhere to be found.

10
December 1, 2011

"Can we play again?" Elsie asked.

"No way! We won fair and square," Kayleigh said, looking at Saryn for confirmation.

"Just one more game, for payback," Griff said, nudging my shoulder with his as we shared each other's space on the floor.

We were having another Game Night, talking, laughing and just being kids, having fun. It helped take my mind off of my mom dying and my dad falling apart. Griff had been coming around for a couple of weeks, ever since Meubles and I had charged into his life that night. We played games, gossiped, watched movies and listened to music while doodling and enjoying ourselves. He was becoming a regular on our Game Nights and, during the week, we would sometimes have a fire at Griff's in the woods.

My friends knew him and accepted him, but they did not know he was homeless and lived in the woods. They just thought he went to the school across town. It was hard keeping this from them, but I didn't know how they would react.

He was my friend, my secret-knower, my confidant. He really was a wise soul. I guess living in a tent in the woods for the last fourteen months on his own would create a wisdom most teens did not have.

He had a great sense of humor, joking with quick-witted one-liners and puns that left you chuckling, despite wanting to hold back because the jokes were so cheesy. He was smart, both academically and worldly. He somehow kept a 4.0 GPA while taking Honors course and not having electricity, computers or internet access at his 'house'. His kindness was unmatched by anyone I had ever met. He was always looking out for me, helping me and my friends, while never saying a bad word about anyone- including Jax and Tyler.

And this paled in comparison to his physical features. His golden eyes, his caramel skin, chiseled cheeks, dimples when he smiled and his dark, curly hair were a package for sure. He would trim his hair on his own, so it always had a messy quality to it, but he wore it well. Tonight, he did not wear his coat. I noticed his arms, tight with muscle, but looking a bit less hairy, almost like the hair was growing back.

"What's going on with your arms?" I hinted, pointing to his arms.

"I was a little self-conscious," he replied with a cool grin, his hair falling just so over his golden eyes.

And he was pushing this hair out of his golden eyes on Game Night when I snapped back to reality.

"Come one, Jess," Saryn said, "It's your turn to guess."

"Sorry," I said, "I was zoning out a bit."

"Thinking about your mom," Kayleigh asked.

"Yea," I lied. "Thinking about my mom."

I put my piece on G 27.

Why was I suddenly thinking of Griff like this? Why was he always on my mind, taking up head space I didn't have to spare? What was wrong with me? My mom was dying and all I can think of is this kid's dimples? What was wrong with me? Was I falling for a homeless kid?

11

December 7, 2011

"So, Tyler has it all planned out," Braylyn was telling Cassie. Today, I was in the third stall, sitting with my feet up, door locked, avoiding the cafeteria. It was just a day I could not do.

"They're gonna go there after school, when he's not there. He is usually hanging out with that weirdo, Jess," Braylyn added.

"Yea, yea...the one whose mom is dying, right?" Cassie asked.

I couldn't believe what I was hearing. Today of all days. We were supposed to go the library, Griff and I. We were going to do out homework there since it was only fourteen degrees outside and studying at his place was not smart. My dad had been on at 'at-home' kick for the last three days. Instead of spending the day at the bar, he was drinking himself silly on the couch, with the curtains closed and the lights off.

I often wondered how Griff could sleep out there when it felt like this. I was also wondering why he decided to shave his arm hair now, when it was freezing outside. But, then again, I think he was hoping he and I would see more of each other, and he was a little self-conscious.

"Yeah," Braylyn said, "He said they were going to 'get the ball rolling', whatever that means." She finished applying her lip plumper in the mirror as I peeked through the cracks, careful not to make a sound.

They both took one last look at themselves in the mirror before they headed back to the cafeteria.

I dropped my right foot. Then, I dropped my left foot.

It was as if they were made of lead, concrete. I couldn't pick them up and move them. I slid them, one at a time, toward the locked door and slowly turned the latch.

What do I do? Do I tell him about it? Do I even know what I am telling him about? What were they up to? I was not sure, but I knew friends help each other and I felt I had to help Griff.

I just wasn't sure if he considered me a friend…or more?

12

December 1, 2011

"So, will I see you later tonight?" he asked as he crept out of Saryn's back door, leaving Game Night.

"Yes, I am sure you will," I assured him, putting my hands against his coat on his chest. "Now, get out of here. I am still mad at you for beating me tonight."

He grabbed my wrists and held them. "Are you definitely coming later?"

"I promise," I said as I looked into his eyes. Damn, those eyes! I got lost looking into them every time. It was like they were cobras, dancing, playing the flute, hypnotizing me.

"Jess," he breathed, releasing my wrists, scratching at his newly-shaven arms, and turning to walk away, "I cannot wait to see you later tonight."

My heart literally leaped in my chest.

He turned around and looked over his shoulder. "I am counting down the time 'til I see you again."

Could this really be happening? Am I really going to fall for this guy?

13

December 21, 2011

It was packed in there. The music was loud, but not bass-thudding, blast your eardrums loud, but loud enough to drown out the laughing, talking and singing.

I was not comfortable there, but, somehow, Kayleigh, Saryn and Elsie had convinced me to go. They claimed it was the type of party that you had to show up for. If you wanted to be known in school, you had to show your face here. I really didn't care, but Griff said he might show up so I thought I would give it a go.

I had not been anywhere since Death Day. My girls thought it would be a good first time out for me. They had been very patient with me, continuing to have Game Nights, but I could tell they were tired of my depression. It had only been twelve days since Death Day, but it had been a very sad week.

So, here I was, at this party, hoping to see Griff and being sad while drinking this awful punch in the red cups. I had a couple of cups so far and was starting to see blurry images, but could still remember Death Day, so I guzzled another cup, hoping to forget.

I had spotted him. He was rubbing his arms, as if he needed to. He was wearing that awful coat. How could he need it? It wasn't that cold right now. But, then again, he did live in the woods and had a perpetual chill in his bones, in his soul, I would guess.

I was not sure if he would show up that night because Tyler and Jax were known to be showing up. But, then again, Griff was different. He reacted so calmly when I told him about what I had heard. I was hoping to manifest a miracle and here it was. He was here.

We made eye contact, and I waved a little. He lifted his cup at me and smiled.

Kayleigh, Saryn, Elsie and I were drinking this awful, throat-burning concoction. We had all had a good deal of this awful drink.

"Look over there," Kayleigh hiccupped, "Look...it's Tyler. He is so hot!"

She hiccupped again and covered her mouth with her hand.

We all turned in shock.

Saryn exclaimed, "If you think Tyler is hot, then you have had too much of this," and she took the cup from Kayleigh's hand.

We all headed toward the hall bathroom.

"Let's go freshen up," Elsie said, guiding Kayleigh by her elbow. We all crammed into the tiny hall bathroom, ushering Kayleigh in there so she wouldn't say anything else that would embarrass herself.

"Don't look at me like that," Kayleigh retorted, hands on her hips, staring at me like I was the one who guided her to the bathroom. "You're the one who likes a homeless kid."

It got silent. Slowly, all eyes turned to me. It was as if the rest of the party ceased to exist and all you could hear was the four of us breathing in this crammed little room.

"What?" I managed to say, "What are you talking about?" I turned away from them as much as I could in this tiny space. How did they know he was homeless?

My cheeks burned a deep crimson and little beads of sweat formed on my hairline. I turned back to them, and they were all smirking. "Come on, Jess," Elsie prodded. "This is us you are talking to. We talk about it all the time..."

"You talk about me?!" I exclaimed. "When? Without me being there?! You talk about me?"

Kayleigh put her arm around my shoulder, "We don't talk about you in a bad way. We talk about how we can all see that you like him...and he likes you, if that matters. You get all gushy and your eyes sparkle when you are talking about him. And when he's here, it's like you are in another zone."

I couldn't believe this. They thought I was ga-ga over him. They knew me so well.

"Ok, ok," I relented. "I might like him...a little bit."

"A little?" Saryn interrupted. "I think you like him more than a little."

I covered my face with my hands.

And admitted another secret to the universe. "Ok, ok, ok. I like him a lot!"

I couldn't wait to get out of this cramped bathroom to go find Griff.

14

December 13, 2011

I remember the gagging stench of flowers causing my eyes to water before the tears started their continuous cycle. They'd flood my cheeks with sobs escaping from my mouth. And then they would disappear, and I couldn't get a tear to fall if I wanted to.

It was an uncontrollable cycle, even as I used the breathing techniques that my counselor had taught me. But I had to make it through. I had to be the strong one.

Dad, however, barely had the strength to stand for over ten minutes at a time. He was pale, gaunt and looked like death had paid him a visit and lingered long after their meeting.

Shaking hands and saying things like, "I know she is no longer hurting," and "She's in a better place," was getting old.

What better place than with her only child? Why couldn't this place, here on Earth, be her place? It was just not fair.

I couldn't bring myself to go to the casket. I couldn't look at her, lying there, eternally still, waxy, ashen and cold. I just couldn't do it.

Numb, shaking and repeating meaningless words, I cycled through my tears, sobbing and then dry, sobbing and then dry.

And then he walked in.

Griff walked in wearing his coat, but it looked like he tried to clean it. His black pants were spotless, and his hair looked freshly trimmed. As soon as we met eyes, his tears swelled in his eyes, threatening to fall over the edge. Then, as he walked toward me, the tears flowed down his chiseled cheeks. He walked toward me.

He started by shaking my hand. Then, he pulled me into strong embrace.

"I am so unbelievably sorry," he said into my hair as he pulled me close, "I am so sorry."

The sobs started wracking my body with grief, shaking, as he held me tight. Tears and snot, once again, left behind on his coat.

It just felt so natural, so right, there in his arms. My grief was becoming his grief. My pain was becoming his pain, shared by him. He was truly someone I was beginning to like and truly appreciated.

His embrace gave me the strength and power to continue through the funeral, delivering the tear-filled words of the eulogy with as much clarity as I could muster.

He sat in the back, listening. The whole time his eyes never left my face.

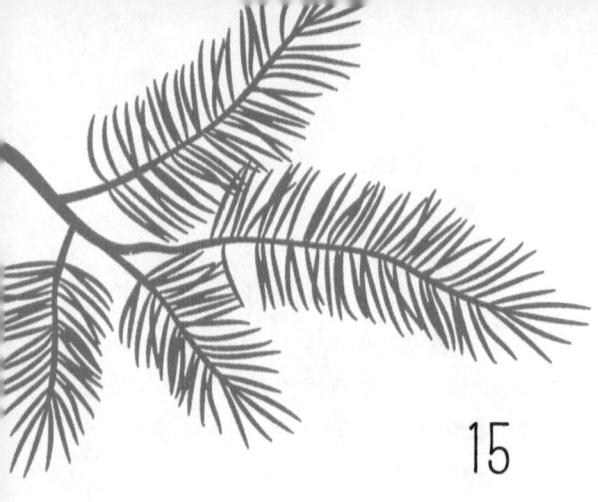

15

December 21, 2011

After about twenty minutes roaming through the rooms, I found Griff outside, getting ready to leave. He was riding a bike.

I must've been drunk because I laughed for about five minutes thinking that him riding a bike was the funniest thing I had ever heard.

When I finally stopped laughing and crying, he wanted to know what my plans were.

"Are you going home tonight or are you sleeping at Kayleigh's house?" he asked, buttoning the last button on his coat.

"I think I am going to get dropped off at home," I said. "Would you want company…hiccup…later," I stammered.

"If you can walk, you are welcome to visit," he replied with a giggle and a shake of his head. "Are you going to be ok? You look a little wasted, no offense."

I giggled, "No offense taken. I am wasted!"

He swung his leg over the bar, "So will I see you later?" he asked.

"I believe...hiccup...you might," I slurred.

And with that, he pedaled off and I turned and returned to the party.

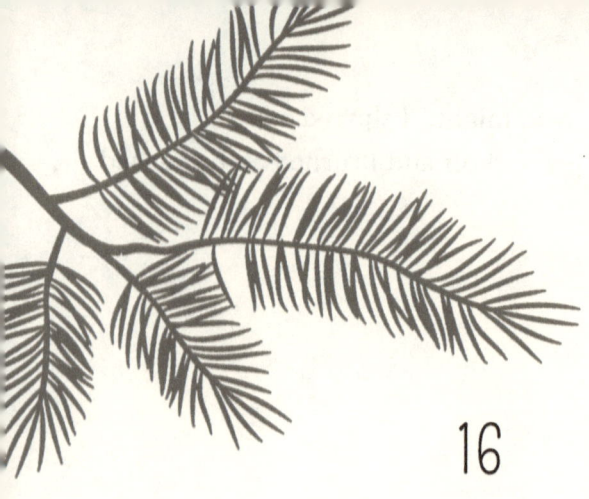

16

December 17, 2011

"You might ask me, 'What is it like having two parents die their own deaths?' and I would ask you, 'What's it like not to have parents?'" I said to Griff one day, sitting on the cooler, facing him sitting on the ground, trying to tie down the tarp.

"And I would ask you, 'What is it like to be such a strong person?' and you might ask me 'Why is it so cold here?'" he said with a laugh.

Man, there wasn't anything I couldn't share with him. He was my confidant, my best friend. He knew everything about me. He knew my deepest fears and my worst nightmares. I had never shared these thoughts with anyone before. I had barely allowed myself to even think of them before.

I was freed from my self-inflicted prison of loneliness. I had shown my true self to someone else, sharing the real me with someone else. There was no turning back on this one. My heart and soul were lost to him.

My heart had welcomed him, gladly opening the door.

"Wipe your feet at the door," my heart said, watching as he trudged through my heart without so much as a glance at the mat.

So, in hindsight, I should have seen the muddy prints being tracked through my heart and known that I would be forever changed by this person.

I just didn't think I would be the type to willingly hold the door open, smiling, inviting someone in to stomp muddy foot prints into my heart.

17

December 23, 2011

"**T**ell me again what happened," my dad said to me as I sat cross-legged leaning against the pillows that used to hold my mother up.

"Dad, this is so hard. Please listen to me, really, really listen to me," I started. "I was walking Meubles and I brought her home. Then, I felt all jittery from the party and went back out by myself." I had to stop and make sure he was with me.

With all the meds he was popping, I wasn't sure how much was getting through to him.

"Dad, he attacked me," I stated, clearly, turning my face to him, showing the bruises around my neck, the cut on my lips, my swollen nose.

He looked at me then, really looked at me, and it was like someone suddenly turned on a light. It was like he had seen me clearly for the first time in months.

"Who did this to you?" he demanded, his fists clenched, holding on to the arms of the chair. "Who attacked you!?"

"I'm pretty sure it was Tyler," I explained. "He had on Griff's coat, but I know he was planning on stealing the coat. So, I am pretty sure it was Tyler. He smelled like Tyler and had sounded like him. And then there was what I had heard. I had heard him and Jax talking about taking 'it'. The 'it', I believed now, was the coat. They tried to frame Griff for this."

I explained how he overtook me, arm wrapped around my neck, everything going black.

"How do you know it's not this weird, homeless kid you have been falling for?" he asked, seeming to know about how I felt about Griff.

"Because…he wouldn't do this. We're friends, good friends, and he wouldn't do that to me."

I paused and added, "So when I heard Cassie and Braylyn talk about it and heard Jax and Tyler talking about taking 'it', I figured it had to be them, trying to frame Griff. They want him to look guilty. They're trying to make it seem like he did this."

I uncrossed my legs and leaned forward, taking my dad's hands.

"Dad, I know it was him. He was setting Griff up. Griff would never hurt me."

18
December 21, 2011

"I'll be back in a bit," I told Meubles as I closed the door. The party was probably still going, but I had to leave. My brain was spinning, and I could barely put words together to make sense as I tried to speak sentences coherently. She whined from behind the door.

"Shhhh, girl, I will be back soon," I whispered, hoping dad was drunk enough to sleep through her whining.

I was keyed up from the party. I had too many drinks. I was still not feeling quite right, but at least the ground wasn't spinning anymore. I couldn't get the idea that my mom was lying under the freshly churned ground, never again to see the light of day.

I walked in solitude. I headed back to the trail and the veered off toward the bridge. I knew where I was heading. I walked toward the center of the woods.

"Griff," I called in a whisper as I approached. "It's me, Jess," I called. This went unanswered. It was eerily quiet. Maybe he wasn't there.

But, why would he not be here? Where else would he be?

Did Jax and Tyler come here? Did they try to take whatever it was they were taking and do something to Griff?

"Griff, it's me," I called again, walking slowly toward the blue tarps.

Just then, I heard a crack behind me. There was the snap of a twig. Something, or someone, was there, behind me, sneaking.

I turned and ran.

19

December 22, 2011

"So, you heard them say they were going to take something from me?" Griff asked, as he studied my bruises and scrapes with a concerned look in his eye and a frown on his face.

I brought my eyes up from the bottom of the tent to meet his gaze.

"Yes, I did. Three days ago, I heard Braylin and Cassie and then a couple days before that I heard Jax and Tyler in the hall and in the cafeteria a week ago.

"They said they were going to take 'it'. But I didn't know what 'it' was. If I figured it out. If I knew what it was, maybe I could have stopped this..."

"Stop that," he interrupted. "You are not at fault for this. They attacked you, Jess...wearing my coat. They set me up for hurting you and that is not okay." He was pacing under the tarp.

It was drizzling so we were talking indoors. This was my first visit since the attack, when I had awoken not far from his tent.

"I know, I know," I replied, shivering, partly from the cold, wet weather and partly from the topic of our intense conversation.

"I'm just so pissed...those...those...jerks! How could they do this?" He was so mad, so angry, horrifyingly abhorred by Jax and Tyler.

He was so mad. He wanted to protect me so badly. He wanted me to feel safe again.

"Don't worry, Jess. It's going to be ok."

20
December 22, 2011

"Honey, are you ok?" my dad asked me, with real, actual concern in his eyes.

It was the first time he had asked me this question since she got sick, since she started dying in front of us. I cannot believe that it took someone attacking me to get him to come back to reality. But, at least he was back, for now.

"No, dad...I mean, yes, I am okay, but no I am not okay," I muddled through my response, trying to stay strong. But it was so hard. Death Day had rocked me to my core. And trying to keep functioning was draining me.

So, this attack...it might be the death of me.

"Dad," I said, snapping back to reality, "I am not going to the police."

"What? No, you are going," he demanded, wringing his hands, "Those jerks need to pay."

"Dad," I said, grabbing his hands, holding them in front of him. "I don't want to be known as the girl who got attacked. And besides, I am ok. Nothing is hurt."

Well, at least not on the outside. My soul is fractured, and my heart is broken into pieces, but, look at me, I will be ok...I think.

"Honey, no," he said, shaking his head. "We need to tell them. We need to let them know what happened. They need to pay! They can't do this to you-or to that homeless boy! They cannot get away with this!" he screamed as he pounded the arms of the chair.

This was the first emotion-this burst- that I had seen since Death Day. I was overcome with emotions. I broke down and sobbed, heaved, retched with tears. My sobs shook my body, and I folded in half.

He swept me into his arms, hugging me, lifting my sadness and pain.

"Honey, I am so sorry, so, so sorry for everything This shouldn't happen to such a good soul," he wept. "I am so, so sorry." We stayed like this for a while. I eventually stopped shuddering, sobbing, heaving the grief out of my body.

"Honey, just one more time," he said, taking my shoulders in his hands. "Just one more time, I need you to be strong. I am here. I will help you." He looked into my eyes, and I was once again overcome.

I couldn't believe he was back, standing here, supporting me.

"I'll think about it, Dad," I said, hugging him. "I'll think about it," I lied, knowing I would never tell what happened.

21
December 23, 2011

"What do you mean, it was in my locker?" Tyler yelled, his face red, shaking his head, pacing in front of the principal's desk. "That can't be! I have no clue where it came from. Someone else had to put it there."

"Tyler, I know this is hard, but why would someone put a coat in your locker?" Mr. Marshall, the principal, asked him. He had already called the police when John, a sophomore on the team, brought the bloodied coat in a bag to him. He said he had found it sticking out of Tyler's locker in the locker room.

"I don't know...maybe they're jealous of me. Maybe someone hates me...maybe someone wants to ruin my life! How would I know?" Tyler sagged into the chair after yelling this. His head went into his hands. "Someone is trying to ruin my life," he started to sob. "I don't know..."

Mr. Marshall sat next to him in a chair. "Tyler, it was in your locked locker. YOUR locker. LOCKED. How else would it have gotten under your practice gear?"

"It wasn't me," he pleaded. "I promise. Why would I have put it in my school locker? That's stupid."

"That's what you would want us to think," Mr. Marshall explained. "That's what the officer said."

Tyler broke into heaving sobs. He was crying and shaking. Mr. Marshall couldn't help but feel bad for this young man whose life was ruined all because of a silly prank.

Yea, Jax and he had talked about taking the coat, but they hadn't done anything yet. They were going to leave it behind and make it look like Griffin had tried to steal some stuff from old lady Wilson's house. But they never got the chance to stage it. This had blind-sided him before they had a chance to even take the darn coat.

There was a knock on the door and then it pushed open.

A police officer walked in and pulled the handcuffs from his belt.

22
December 24, 2011

He was pacing as I walked up to the tent- he always seemed to be pacing when he was here. It was like he was a wild animal.

"I came by to tell you that Kayleigh, Elsie and Saryn told me that they found your coat," I started.

"What? Where? I need that back!" he responded at once.

"...and say Merry Christmas," I finished. "Get this...it was in his locker. He balled it up, stuffed it in a trash bag and put it in his locker. It had...ummmm...it had...my blood on it still, crusted and stuff," I couldn't bring myself to look him in the eyes.

"Well, that's pretty stupid," he declared and stopped pacing, "I didn't even think he was that stupid."

"Tell me about it," I agreed. "I am just glad that they found it before he could get rid of it. It just proves they were setting you up...that they did this to me."

He took three steps and closed the space between us. He wrapped me tightly in his arms. They were soft with fresh hair.

He pulled back from me and looked me in the eyes.

"They put him in the back of the cop car, in cuffs is what they were telling me," I managed to explain.

"I can't say that I feel bad for him," he said, staring into my soul with those damn golden eyes. "Did you tell anyone else about the coat and them finding it in his locker?"

He squeezed me tight again.

"I don't need to. Everyone is talking about it. I almost wish it had not happened at school because then I wouldn't have to do anything about it."

He took my hand and led me to his tent. We sat side by side on top of his closed cooler, the one that doubled as a chair.

"I think you need to go to the police," he said, holding my hand in his. It felt so warm, so right, so safe. "I think that they need to know what you heard Jax and Tyler saying and that you think they are responsible for attacking you."

My heart hurt when he said those words- 'attacking you.' I cannot fully believe that they did this to me. Why would they want to attack me and make it look like Griff did it? How could they be so cold? So heartless?

His eyes softened the pain in my chest. It looked as though he were trying to take some of the pain away from my heart, my soul.

We sat, with the words 'you need to go to the police' lingering between us like electricity. I swear I felt my skin zap with it when his hand rested on my knee. I felt warm from his touch and wanted him to wrap his other arm around my shoulder and pull me close.

Instead, he looked deep into my eyes and said, "Jax and Tyler need to pay for what they have done."

23

December 24, 2011

Dad and I were having lunch in the kitchen. We were eating his favorite, egg salad sandwich with potato chips, and there was a knock on the door.

Officer Clark stood outside with Officer Kirkson behind him.

"Hi there, Jess," he said, looking past me to my father, who still sat in the kitchen.

"Jess, who's there?" he hollered.

"It's the officers, Dad," I yelled back, inviting them in.

"Jess, ummm, some people have been talking about where you go those bruises and scrapes from and then there's this bloody coat that turns up and Tyler Lockhold is at the station yelling that it's some homeless kid...some kid named Griffin something or other...and he said you knew where this kid 'lived'," he put these in air quotes, "And that maybe you knew who had done this to you but weren't saying anything."

Officer Kirkson stepped forward at this point and she grabbed my hands and held them in front of me, "Honey, it's not okay for someone to do that to you. Don't feel bad for him because he's homeless. He hurt you. He needs to be held accountable for his actions," she explained this to me as if I thought that Griff would ever hurt a hair on my head.

"M'am, with all due respect, you are incorrect. Griff would never do anything to hurt me. He is my friend, my confidante..." and here came those tears again. "Officers, let me tell you what I know."

And I told them the whole story.

24
December 25, 2011

Griff walked toward me. He was wearing, of course, the coat. It had been cleaned, but he refused another one. I found out it had belonged to his dad and that's why he wanted it back so badly. I also found out what a great kisser he was.

"I was so scared for a bit," he told me, wrapping his arm over my shoulders. "I didn't know if you were going to tell the police or not. I didn't want to pressure you, but I am sure glad that you did. I don't think they would have arrested and charged Tyler if not."

"I know," I replied, as we walked toward his tent. "I am not sure if my testimony is enough. I was drunk and it was dark. I never got a great look at his face. But his arms were wiry, and he had that silly tattoo on his wrist. You know, then one with the road runner and the football?"

"Yea, I know the one," Griff replied, scratching at his wrist. "You just have to sound confident. Just say you caught a glimpse of him in the light. Really, who will know?" He smiled at me. He wanted me to be happy. He just wanted me to feel safe.

Tyler was charged and would hopefully be behind bars and I was here, with Griff.

I was a lucky girl.

Here I was, spending Christmas with someone so amazing, someone I was certainly falling for.

"Here," he said, handing me a small box. "It's not much, but it's special to me."

I opened it and saw the beautiful angel pendant.

"It was my mom's," he said. "She wanted me to give it to someone special, and well," he scratched at his freshly trimmed hair. "Well, I think you are pretty special."

25
Griff
December 25, 2011

I cannot believe this worked out like it did. This was almost too easy. After she told me about those two idiots wanting to take my coat, it was too easy to convince her it was them, to design a plan to set them up instead.

And, the icing on the cake is that Tyler got to take the fall for both of them. He was the only one being charged and held without bail...and all because of what I did.

Talk about getting away with it.

I just had to make sure she never found out it was me.

Jess turned and smiled at me with the pendant in her hand and tears in her eyes.

That look of love felt so amazing.

"I'll never tell," I thought to myself. "I'll never tell."

Discussion Questions

1. What do you think the most pivotal part of the story was? Why do you say this?

2. Compare yourself to Jess or Griff. How are you similar to and different from this character?

3. Why do you think the author chose to tell the story out of order? How did this help your understanding or hurt your understanding of the story's events?

4. Explain how Jess is an unreliable character. Why would the author want to create a main character that is unreliable? How does that impact the story for the reader?

5. Which minor character had the biggest, most impactful role? Why do you say this?

6. What life lessons can you learn from the characters in the story? Do you see this more in the characters' words, thoughts, or actions?

7. Describe what you think Jess's and Griff's lives were like before they met. Why do you think their lives were like this?

8. If you could write a sequel to this story, what would happen to Jess and Griff?

9. Imagine you could write about one night that changed your life, which night would you write about? How did this change your life?

10. What would be a better title for this book? Why is this title a better title?

About the Author

Jessaka lives in Ocean View, DE with her two sons, Britan, Caden, and her two daughters, Ellery and Kinley. Ellery and Kinley have co-authored children's picture books with their mom. They are called "Animal Family Adventures: First Time Family" and "Finally Home...Alone." She also lives with her dog, Doodie, (who makes an appearance in a book) and two cats, Kitty Purry and Meebles.

She is a Language Arts teacher, finishing her twenty-third year of public-school teaching in a variety of schools, districts and states. She has taught all grades, from first through high school, and has made it (so far) to tell the tale. Her students and their experiences helped to create some of the characters in the stories that are already in print, and those that are yet to be told.

She loves reading mystery and true crime books and authoring her own stories while not teaching. She practices yoga and runs in her spare time, while creating courses for personal reflection, meditation, and growth.

Check out her site www.jessakanastalski.com for more information.